Under Cover of Darkness

by

Pat Thomson

Illustrated by Kevin Hopgood

For Paula – champion of poetry and people.

With special thanks to:

James Brannan

First published in 2009 in Great Britain by
Barrington Stoke Ltd
18 Walker St, Edinburgh, EH3 7LP

www.barringtonstoke.co.uk

ISBN: 978-1-84299-778-9

Printed in Great Britain by Bell & Bain Ltd

Contents

This is a story, but it is based on real events. There were young people working in secret for the Resistance in Europe during the 1939-45 war.

Chapter 1
Shadows

Michel stood still in the dark. He could hear the drone of a single plane overhead.

"One plane," he said to himself. "Small. Not a bomber. Something's up."

Nico growled softly. He was a clever dog and Michel's father had trained him well.

"Shh, Nico!" said Michel. Nico stood still.

The boy moved to the edge of the forest.
He stayed hidden, but he could now see the
sky. The moon was very bright, but they
had to fly on moonlit nights. The plane
needed light to see its target. It was flying
over the mountain. On the far side, it was
wild. Truly wild. He knew men were hiding
out there.

The Nazis had taken over France but they had not won. The French were still fighting. Resisting the enemy, they called it. Michel wanted, more than anything, to join one of these Resistance groups and fight the Germans.

It seemed, however, that he was too young to do anything, even though he was nearly thirteen. That's what his mum said. He just watched. He watched most nights.

As the plane moved through the air, its shadow travelled along the ground below it. The plane was flying high and its shadow skimmed the green hills below. Then, he saw a flash of white.

"Not search lights," he said softly to himself. "Please!"

No. The flash of white was a parachute! He saw it coming down on the mountain top.

Then he saw another. It must be a British plane. The British and the French were fighting the Nazis together. The Royal Air Force, the RAF, were helping the French by dropping supplies like guns and radios to the people in the hills. He wanted to be there, doing something to help.

Then he couldn't see the plane any more. It had gone behind the mountain.

Time to go home before Mum woke. She would go mad if she knew where he was. He grinned to himself.

Michel's house was at the edge of the village. He knew the forest well. It started

at his gate and went right up to the foothills
of the big mountain. Most nights, he
climbed out of his bedroom window, down
the apple tree and went out of the gate. No
one heard him, no one knew where he was.

He stopped for a moment between the trees and listened. Nico stood still beside him. Nothing. He went on.

Of course Mum was afraid. His father had joined the army. At first, he sent letters. Then, about three months ago, there had been a terrible battle. Almost everyone had been killed, they said. There had been no news of his father.

"We must always hope," Mum had said, but she had cried.

He stopped again at the edge of the forest. All clear. In a few moments, he was closing his gate.

He had oiled it. Clever boy!

Nico ran silently to his kennel. Good dog!

Michel went up the apple tree. Easy!

In by the open window. No problem!

The chair on the other side of his room was in deep shadow. Then, quite slowly, the shadow moved.

Chapter 2
The Enemy

"And where have you been?" It was Mum and she was angry. She spoke softly and he knew she was trying not to wake his little sister, Anne. "Don't you know how much I have to worry about already?" Her fingers drummed on the bedside table. "Where have you been?"

"Just out to watch. I heard a plane. Something's going on."

"Of course something is 'going on'," snapped Mum. "It's a war, stupid child."

"I'm not a child!" He tried not to shout. A child would shout.

"No," said Mum. "You are at a tricky age. Too young for the army but old enough to be in danger."

"What do you mean?"

"The news is bad. The Nazis are on their way to this village. It will be difficult for boys your age. You will be a suspect."

"What will they think I'm up to?" Michel stared at her.

"Everything," she sighed, "from being rude to German soldiers to damaging their gear. You could be shot for either." She turned away and then stopped in the doorway and looked back at Michel. "I have a lot to worry about, Michel. I have two children to feed on less and less food and I don't even know if Dad is alive."

She picked up a little carved wooden dog from Michel's bedside table. It was Nico, of course. Dad had carved it. He was clever at carving animals.

Then they both heard a loud rumbling noise. It sounded like the roar of engines. It sounded like a rattling that went on and on.

Mum dashed out of the room and up the attic stairs. Michel ran after her. She was standing at the highest window in the house. They were in a big store room that still had the smell of apples from last year. From the window, they could just see the market place.

Wave after wave of lorries and jeeps were pouring into the village. They could see the dimmed side lights and could tell from the change of sound when the big trucks hit the cobbles.

It's the Nazis," said Mum. "They will be all over the village tomorrow. There is nothing we can do. Go to bed."

Michel went back to his room. He went
over to the window and stood staring at
nothing. Below him, Nico whined. Michel
leaned out. Then he heard something odd.
Mum was out there talking softly to Nico.

She passed the kennel and went to the old woodshed. The woodshed? In the middle of the night? He waited but she did not come out again.

He sat on his bed. Something was happening and even his mum was mixed up in it.

Chapter 3
The Warning

The next day was awful. There were Nazi soldiers everywhere. Michel crossed the road and went into school. There was only one classroom and the teacher was old Mr Norbert. All the younger teachers were in the army. Or with the Resistance in the hills. Mr Norbert carried on teaching as if everything was normal.

One of the younger boys put his hand up. "Sir, sir, is it true that there was a parachute drop last night? Did the RAF drop someone?"

"Goodness," replied Mr Norbert, "How would I know? An old man needs his sleep. I can sleep through anything."

He was writing out long sums on the
board when the door banged open. A Nazi
officer stood in the doorway. Behind him
were two soldiers. Both had guns.

"Good morning," said Mr Norbert in a weak voice. He stood hunched and old. That was odd. Mr Norbert was old but he always stood up tall – and his voice had never been weak before – as Michel knew well!

The officer did not reply. He slapped his gloves on a desk and looked at the sums on the board.

"Number work," he said, in French. "Good." He walked round the class, flicking some children with his gloves. "Stick to your school work," he said, "and you will be safe. Don't get in my way or I shall think you are my enemy. Remember, I shoot my enemies."

"Dear, dear," said old Mr Norbert. "That would never do!" He limped round the desk and waved at the children. "These are such good little ones."

"Some are not so little," replied the officer and looked at the back row. Michel made himself stare back. "Anyway, they have had their warning. Stay off the street after dark. We shoot at sight."

The man swaggered out. One of the soldiers shut the door and the class relaxed.

"Be careful," said Mr Norbert. "All of you. They will shoot you if they feel like it. They have already done that in other places." He walked back to the board. "Let's get on," he said with a sigh and a yawn.

Michel looked at him. He was tall again. He seemed to have lost his limp. Why had he tried to make the officer think he was so feeble? Now he came to think of it, Mr Norbert was often worn out in the morning.

Sometimes he could hardly keep his eyes open.

But then, thought Michel, what could Mr Norbert do? He was old.

Chapter 4
A Knock on the Door

After school, Mum wanted some jobs done in the garden. They stood looking at the rows of vegetables. "We must grow as much food for ourselves as possible," she explained. "Pick anything that's ready and we will store it. No need to tell everyone

what we've got," she added as she went
indoors.

Perhaps it was food that Mum had in the
old woodshed. Was she hiding it from the
enemy in there?

He peeped through the kitchen window.
She was busy feeding little Anne. He went

at once to the woodshed and opened the door. He looked round but could see nothing except wood. There was a trap-door in the roof and he went up the ladder. The roof space was full of boxes. Nothing else.

They ate their soup in silence that night until his mother said, "Please, Michel, don't go out tonight. There's danger out there. The soldiers are everywhere."

He nodded. He was a school boy, but that would not save him from being shot. The Nazi officer had meant what he said.

Suddenly, Nico got up and stood looking at the door. He whined softly and then barked and ran to the door. There was someone there.

There were four knocks. Three soft, one louder. A signal!

Michel's mother ran to open the door.

"Only me." It was George, a friend of his father's. Michel knew Mum trusted George. He put a small packet of meat on the kitchen table. "Dinner for the children with no father," he said and then put a finger to his lips. "And a little present for the baby," he added and took something out of his pocket. "For little Anne, and with love to you all from the person who made it."

Mum took it, staring at it. She was holding a tiny wooden rabbit. It could only have been made by Dad.

"Don't ask me where it came from."

George smiled, then winked. "Must go now.

Other jobs. You know how it is."

"Goodnight," said Mum. "And George,

thank you. Thank you for everything."

When the door was shut and bolted, Mum hugged Michel. "Dad's alive," she said softly.

"Dad's still fighting, isn't he? In the hills."

"We must never tell anyone. If they ask, he's in the army. We don't know where."

"I want to do something," said Michel. "I want to help the secret army. I want to join the Resistance."

"Ssh!" replied Mum, and put a hand over his mouth. "Never speak of it. Anyway, you are too young."

I'm not too young to do something, thought Michel. I'm going to fight. Somehow.

Chapter 5
Night Visitors

But all Michel had to fight against were the weeds in the vegetable garden. The food shops in the village were closing one by one so he knew it was important to look after the garden. But this wasn't what he really wanted to do.

Two nights later, there was a raid. Overhead, bombers flew on an unending wave of sound. Soon, they heard the anti-aircraft guns. Mum, with Anne sleeping in her arms, came and stood at Michel's window.

They saw bombs exploding, but some way away. Then they heard a terrible screeching noise.

"That's a plane coming down." Michel looked at Mum.

The next moment, the ground shook. It was close.

"It's come down in the forest," said Mum.

Michel watched until nearly dawn. He began to yawn – and then stood very still. Someone was knocking on the door. Three soft knocks, then one loud one. Nico had not barked.

Michel looked down into the garden. There were two men. One was wearing a bulky jacket. A flying jacket. And Mum was

taking them into the woodshed.

Soon Mum came out. There was only one man now and he melted into the shadows of the forest.

Michel ran down to the kitchen. Mum was putting some bread and ham in a basket. She added a bottle of water and some wine.

"I saw you," he said.

"Then I must trust you, Michel." Mum was very calm. "You understand, Michel? This man's life depends on us. When it is safe, Mr Norbert will come and take him up into the hills."

"Mr Norbert? Old Mr Norbert?" Michel was amazed.

Mum smiled. "Mr Norbert is not the person you think he is. He's sent many RAF men safely back to England. Keep a look-out while I take this over to the woodshed."

He heard her moving wood in the woodshed. She came out smiling. "I've told him he'll only be a day or two in there. We must wait until the fuss dies down."

"Is the hiding place under the woodshed? I thought it was in the roof. I didn't see anything on the floor."

"No one must see anything. I hid the second trap-door well." They both smiled. Now they could help each other.

They were not happy for long. The next morning, school was closed. "Poor old Norbert's in hospital," someone told them.

Chapter 6
The Dogs of War

Mum came back from the hospital looking upset. "A broken ankle and burns on his hands. He says he tripped and knocked the lamp over."

"Is it true?"

Mum shook her head. "When the plane crashed, he rescued two men. One came to us. He's the man in the woodshed."

"But what do we do now?" asked Michel.

Mum said nothing at first. She looked at Michel. "Mr Norbert says you can do his job."

"Me?" Michel was amazed – and scared.

"I told him you were too young but he says you know the forest as well as he does. Then, he said he trusted you. He said you can do it." Mum looked at him. "Can you

get our man as far as the river? Someone
would meet you there. Can you do it?"

"Of course I can," said Michel.

That night, Michel and the airman
slipped into the forest. Nico padded behind.
Michel chose his paths with care and they
met no one. He began to relax a little when
they were over half way to the river.

But then, Nico whined.

Voices far off.

Cracking twigs.

Flashing lights.

There was someone there. And voices speaking German.

Michel pulled the airman behind a tree. "We have to get past them," he said in a low voice. "There's no other way now."

The man shrugged. "You're in charge," he said to Michel.

Michel felt sick.

They lay under a bush and listened. The soldiers were not going away again. They were searching around, coming closer. Suddenly, everything seemed loud. Michel could hear the airman breathing. His own heart sounded like a big, wild drum. And, to his horror, he could hear a kind of snuffling.

The Nazi soldiers had dogs with them.

Michel had to decide fast. "We must risk it!" he said.

"Something here!" yelled one of the Nazi soldiers.

At that moment, Nico burst out of the bushes, barking like mad. He threw himself on the leading dog and the forest exploded.

"A dog! Deal with it!" That must be the Nazi officer.

"Now!" Michel and the airman ran at top speed through the trees. Behind them a

single shot rang out. "Not Nico!" gasped
Michel, but they had to keep going until they
made it to the river. As they lay on the
river bank, panting, someone whistled.
Three short whistles and a long one. Three
shadows came out of the darkness. One was
wearing an RAF uniform.

"Well done, lad," said a voice he knew. "You're coming back with me now." It was George.

The next morning, Michel came home on George's cart, hidden under some vegetables. As he walked through his gate, the door opened and Mum rushed out.

Behind her was Nico. He looked battered but pleased with himself.

Like a dog that had been in a fight – and won!

They Shall Not Pass

by
Andy Croft

Sam is Jewish. His friend Alf is Irish. At first that didn't matter.
But now the Black Shirts want to get rid of the Jews – and Alf is on their side. Now Sam has to fight for what's right ...

You can order *They Shall Not Pass* from our website at
www.barringtonstoke.co.uk

The Dunkirk Escape

by
Jim Eldridge

Dave Jones is trapped on the beach at Dunkirk, as bombs explode all around him. Can his son Tom get there in time to save him?

You can order *The Dunkirk Escape* from our website at www.barringtonstoke.co.uk

Lucky

by
S. P. Gates

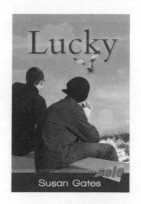

Everyone thinks because Dom is big, he's a bully. But Leon knows what he's really like. And when an injured seagull needs their help, Leon finds out there's even more to Dom than he thought ...

You can order *Lucky* from our website at
www.barringtonstoke.co.uk

Killer Croc

by
S. P. Gates

Levi is in danger.
There's a killer croc on the loose – and it's
hungry! Can he escape its jaws?

You can order *Killer Croc* from our website at
www.barringtonstoke.co.uk

Cliff Edge

by
Jane A. C. West

Can Danny make the climb of his life to save his friend?
No ropes, no help – no hope?

You can order *Cliff Edge* from our website at
www.barringtonstoke.co.uk